Legends of the Guardian Stone

The Guardian Stone, Volume 1

Sable Moonshadow

Published by AUMANGEA GROUP LIMITED, 2024.

Chapter 1: The Ordinary World Beginning:

Liora stood at the edge of the Vyrn Forest, the scent of pine and earth mingling with the delicate aroma of the herbs she had just collected. The morning sun filtered through the dense canopy, casting dappled shadows on the forest floor. She adjusted the leather strap of her satchel, heavy with freshly gathered plants, and sighed deeply.

Her village, Eldergrove, was a quaint collection of thatched cottages and cobblestone paths. Nestled against the boundary of the enchanted Vyrn Forest, it thrived on the bounty of the woods and the skill of its inhabitants. Liora's family had been herbalists for generations, their knowledge of the forest's flora passed down through time. She had inherited her mother's keen sense for finding the rarest herbs and her father's gentle touch in crafting potent remedies.

Every morning, Liora began her day with a walk into the forest, her senses alert for the telltale signs of useful plants. She would return to her family's apothecary shop, a cozy place filled with the scents of dried herbs and the soft glow of sunlight through stained glass windows. Here, she would spend hours sorting, drying, and preparing her finds, creating tinctures, balms, and teas to cure the villagers' ailments.

Despite the tranquil rhythm of her days, a restlessness gnawed at Liora's heart. She longed for something more than the familiar paths of Eldergrove and the predictable cycles of the seasons. The stories her grandmother told her as a child—tales of ancient magic, brave heroes, and distant lands—stirred a yearning for adventure within her. She often found herself daydreaming as she worked, imagining herself as the heroine of her own epic saga.

Today was no different. As she crushed a handful of dried lavender, her thoughts drifted to the legends of the Guardian Stone, a mythical artifact said to protect the land from dark forces. She had heard whispers in the village of shadows creeping at the forest's edge, unsettling rumors that made her wonder if there was some truth to the old tales.

As she worked, Liora's mind raced with possibilities. The whispers of the Guardian Stone and the growing shadows at the forest's edge filled her with a sense of anticipation. Maybe this was the adventure she had been waiting for. With renewed energy, she continued her work, her thoughts now filled with the promise of the unknown.

As the sun dipped lower in the sky, casting a golden hue over Eldergrove, Liora set out toward the forest. Her satchel swung lightly at her side, filled with the essentials she might need. The path she took was one she had walked countless times, but today it felt different, charged with a sense of purpose and mystery.

Liora's steps were sure and confident as she moved deeper into the Vyrn Forest. The air grew cooler and the light dimmer, filtered through the thick canopy above. She paused occasionally to gather herbs, her hands moving deftly to pick the right leaves and flowers. She knew every plant by sight, smell, and touch, her fingers brushing over the soft petals and rough stems with practiced ease.

The forest was alive with the sounds of chirping birds, rustling leaves, and the distant trickle of a stream. Liora felt a profound connection to this place, as if the forest itself recognized her as one of its own. She often spoke to the plants and animals as she worked, a habit that brought her comfort and made the solitude of her task feel less lonely.

As she ventured further, she found herself in a part of the forest she seldom visited. Ancient trees with massive trunks and gnarled roots dominated the landscape. It was here, among these venerable giants, that she hoped to find the rarest herbs. She knelt beside a patch of luminous moonwort, its silvery leaves glowing faintly in the fading light. Just as she was about to pick a handful, something caught her eye.

Beneath the roots of a colossal oak, a faint, otherworldly glow pulsed gently. Liora's curiosity piqued, she pushed aside the ferns and underbrush, revealing a hollow beneath the tree. She reached in, her fingers brushing against something smooth and cool. With a gentle tug, she pulled it free.

It was an amulet, ancient and intricately designed, with a large, glowing gemstone at its center. The light emanating from it was mesmerizing, a soft, ethereal blue that seemed to dance and shimmer. Liora held it up, examining the delicate patterns etched into the metal. It felt warm in her hand, as if it had a life of its own.

A sense of awe and wonder filled her. The amulet was unlike anything she had ever seen, its beauty and craftsmanship far beyond anything the villagers could create. She wondered who had left it here and what purpose it might serve. The old tales of magic and guardians whispered through her mind, and she couldn't shake the feeling that she had stumbled upon something of great importance.

Her heart pounded with excitement and a hint of trepidation. A part of her wanted to keep this discovery to herself, to unravel its secrets alone. The forest around her seemed to hold its breath, as if watching and waiting for her decision.

Carefully, she placed the amulet into her satchel, its glow fading slightly as it disappeared from view. She stood up, brushing the dirt from her hands and clothes, and continued her journey. The forest, once familiar and comforting, now felt like a place of untold possibilities and hidden wonders.

As she made her way back, Liora's mind raced with questions. What was the amulet's origin? Why had it been hidden beneath the roots of an ancient tree? And most importantly, what role would it play in the adventure she felt was now undeniably beginning?

The sun had nearly set by the time she reached the edge of the forest. Liora paused, her heart pounding with anticipation. She could feel the weight of the amulet in her satchel, its presence almost palpable against her side.

With trembling hands, Liora reached into her satchel and retrieved the amulet. The moment it emerged, its glow intensified, casting a soft blue light over her face.

"This is no ordinary amulet," she murmured, her voice filled with a mix of awe and apprehension.

As she held the amulet up, its glow pulsing in response to her touch, a strange sensation washed over her, a tingling warmth spreading from her fingers through her entire body. She felt compelled to close her eyes and focus on the amulet's light.

In an instant, the world around her dissolved. She was no longer standing at the forest's edge but floating in a vast expanse of darkness. Shapes and colors swirled around her, forming a vision that was both vivid and terrifying.

She saw a shadowy figure, cloaked in darkness, its eyes burning with malevolent fire. The figure stood atop a hill, overlooking a land shrouded in gloom. Villages lay in ruins, their inhabitants fleeing in terror from monstrous creatures that seemed to spring from the very shadows themselves. The once-lush forests were now twisted and barren, and the rivers ran black with corruption.

The vision shifted, and Liora found herself facing a dark figure. It raised a hand, and she felt a surge of cold, oppressive power wash over her. She heard a voice, deep and echoing, filled with malice and hunger.

"Return the amulet, or face the wrath of the Shadow Lord. The Guardian Stone will fall, and darkness will reign."

Liora gasped, her eyes snapping open. She was back in the forest, clutching the amulet tightly, her heart pounding in her chest.

"What did I see?" she whispered to herself, her voice trembling.

The vision played back in her mind: a dark force, a figure cloaked in shadows, villages destroyed, people fleeing. It called itself the Shadow Lord. It was coming for the amulet and wanted to destroy the Guardian Stone.

Liora's expression grew grave. The darkness she had sensed at the forest's edge was real, and it was growing stronger. She knew she had to act quickly. The amulet had chosen her for a reason.

Her resolve hardened. The vision had shown her the stakes, the danger that threatened not just her village but the entire land. She knew now that her longing for adventure had been a premonition, a call to a higher purpose.

"What do I do?" she asked herself, determination shining in her eyes.

She placed a hand on her shoulder, as if to reassure herself. "I must seek out the Guardian Stone and protect it at all costs. I am the key. I will face this darkness and restore the light."

As the last rays of the setting sun disappeared behind the trees, Liora felt a sense of destiny settle over her. The ordinary world she had known was slipping away, and in its place, a grand adventure was unfolding. She was ready to embrace it, to fight for her village, her home, and the light that still lingered in the depths of the Vyrn Forest.

Chapter 2: The Call to Adventure

With the amulet safely tucked away in her satchel, Liora made her way back to Eldergrove. The village was bathed in the soft glow of evening lanterns, casting a warm, welcoming light over the cobblestone streets. Despite the calm exterior, Liora felt a storm brewing within her, a mix of fear and determination.

She headed to the home of Mara, the village elder. Mara's cottage was nestled at the edge of the village, surrounded by a garden bursting with vibrant flowers and herbs. The old woman was known for her wisdom and deep knowledge of the ancient lore that bound the village and the forest together.

Liora found Mara sitting on her porch, her gray hair pulled back into a neat bun and her eyes sharp with intelligence. She looked up as Liora approached, her expression softening when she saw her.

"Good evening, Liora," she greeted, her voice gentle but firm. "What brings you here at this hour?"

Liora stepped forward, her face serious. "Mara, I have something important to show you." She carefully retrieved the amulet and handed it to Mara.

The elder's eyes widened as she took the glowing amulet into her hands. She turned it over, studying the intricate patterns and the pulsating light. "By the gods," she whispered, her voice filled with awe. "This is the Amulet of Eldara, the key to the Guardian Stone."

Liora leaned in, her curiosity piqued. "Mara, what do you know about the amulet? And what is the Guardian Stone?"

Mara's gaze shifted from the amulet to Liora. "The Guardian Stone is an ancient artifact, imbued with powerful magic that has protected our land for centuries. It has the ability to repel dark forces and maintain the balance of light and shadow. The amulet you found is a key, one of the few that can unlock the Guardian Stone's true power."

Liora's heart raced. "And the vision I had... It showed a dark figure, the Shadow Lord. He wants to destroy the Guardian Stone."

Mara's face grew grim. "The Shadow Lord is a malevolent force from the old legends, a being of pure darkness and corruption. If he gains control of the Guardian Stone, our world will fall into shadow."

Liora nodded. "That's why I came to you, Mara. I need to know how to find the Guardian Stone and protect it."

Mara closed her eyes for a moment, as if gathering her thoughts. When she opened them again, they shone with resolve. "The path to the Guardian Stone is fraught with danger and challenges. It lies deep within the Vyrn Forest, hidden and protected by powerful enchantments. Only those with a pure heart and strong will can reach it."

Liora felt a shiver run down her spine. "What must I do, Mara?"

The elder took a deep breath. "You must embark on a quest to find the Guardian Stone. The amulet will guide you, revealing the way when the time is right. Along the journey, you will face many trials, but you must stay true to your purpose."

Liora nodded, her resolve firming. "I understand. I'm ready to do whatever it takes to protect our village and the land."

Mara smiled, a glimmer of pride in her eyes. "You have a brave heart, Liora. But remember, you will not be alone. Kael, the village's most experienced ranger, will accompany you on this journey. He has spent years exploring the depths of the Vyrn Forest and has faced countless dangers. His knowledge of the land, his tracking skills, and his prowess in combat will be invaluable to you."

She continued, "Kael has a deep understanding of the forest's secrets and the creatures that dwell within. He has navigated treacherous paths, faced ancient guardians, and emerged victorious. His wisdom and guidance will help you overcome the challenges that lie ahead."

Liora nodded, feeling a sense of reassurance. "I am grateful that Kael will be by my side. His experience and skills will be a great asset."

Mara's expression grew serious. "But remember, Liora, this journey will test you both physically and mentally. You must rely on each other's strengths and trust in the bond you share. Together, you have the power to protect the Guardian Stone and save our land from the Shadow Lord's darkness."

As the gravity of her task settled over her, Liora felt a mixture of fear and excitement. The call to adventure had been sounded, and there was no turning back. With the amulet as their guide and the support of her companions, she was ready to embark on the journey that would shape her destiny and the fate of the land.

Liora sat in Mara's cozy cottage, the amulet glowing softly on the table before her. The elder's words echoed in her mind, the weight of the quest settling heavily on her shoulders. She had always longed for adventure, but now that it was within her grasp, doubt and fear clouded her thoughts.

Mara's wise eyes studied Liora's face. "I understand that this is a daunting task, Liora. But you must believe in yourself. The amulet chose you for a reason."

Liora sighed, her hands trembling slightly as she reached for the amulet. "I don't know if I'm ready for this, Mara. I'm just a herbalist. How can I possibly face the dangers that lie ahead?"

Mara leaned forward, her voice gentle but firm. "You are more than just a herbalist, Liora. You have a deep connection with nature and a pure heart. These qualities will serve you well on your journey. And remember, you will not be alone. Kael will guide you."

Liora looked up, her eyes filled with uncertainty. "Kael... He's so experienced, so strong. What if I let him down? What if I can't do this?"

Mara smiled warmly. "Kael has great respect for you, Liora. He sees the potential within you, just as I do. You have already proven your bravery by finding the amulet and coming to me. Trust in yourself, and trust in Kael's guidance."

Taking a deep breath, Liora nodded slowly. "Alright. I'll find Kael and ask for his help. But... how do I start?"

Mara stood, retrieving a small pouch from a shelf. She handed it to Liora, the contents jingling softly. "This pouch contains a map and some herbs that will aid you on your journey. Follow the path marked on the map to find Kael. He often patrols the deeper parts of the Vyrn Forest. Show him the amulet and explain everything."

Liora took the pouch, her fingers brushing over the worn leather. "Thank you, Mara. I'll do my best."

As she left Mara's cottage, the evening air felt cool against her skin. The village was quiet, the comforting sounds of nightfall enveloping her. Despite her doubts, Liora felt a spark of determination ignite within her. She would find Kael, and together, they would face whatever challenges lay ahead.

The next morning, Liora set out early, the map clutched in her hand and the amulet safely tucked into her satchel. The path through the forest was familiar, but the deeper she ventured, the more foreign it became. The trees grew taller and thicker, their branches intertwining to form a dense canopy overhead. Shafts of sunlight pierced through the leaves, casting dappled shadows on the forest floor.

Liora's senses were on high alert, her eyes scanning the surroundings for any sign of Kael. Her footsteps were quiet, her years of foraging in the forest teaching her how to move silently and avoid disturbing the wildlife. She paused occasionally to examine the map, ensuring she was on the right track.

As the sun climbed higher, Liora's confidence began to waver. The forest seemed endless, and doubts crept back into her mind. What if she couldn't find Kael? What if she got lost and never returned? She shook her head, trying to dispel the negative thoughts.

Just as she was about to take another step, a rustle in the bushes made her freeze. Her heart pounded as she reached for her small knife, the only weapon she had. A figure emerged from the underbrush, and Liora's grip on the knife tightened until she recognized the familiar, weathered face of Kael.

"Kael!" she exclaimed, relief flooding her voice.

Kael raised an eyebrow, a hint of a smile playing on his lips. "Liora? What are you doing out here?"

Liora took a deep breath, her voice steadying. "I need your help, Kael. I found something in the forest—an amulet. Mara says it's the key to finding the Guardian Stone. There's a dark force threatening our land, and I've had a vision of a Shadow Lord. Mara believes I'm meant to protect the Guardian Stone, but I can't do it alone."

Kael's expression turned serious as he listened. "Show me the amulet."

Liora pulled the amulet from her satchel, its soft glow illuminating their faces. Kael examined it closely, his eyes narrowing.

"This is no ordinary amulet," he said quietly. "Mara is right. This is a powerful artifact. And if what you say about the Shadow Lord is true, we don't have much time."

Liora nodded, her earlier doubts fading as Kael's confidence bolstered her own. "Will you help me, Kael? I can't do this without you."

Kael placed a reassuring hand on her shoulder. "Of course, Liora. We'll face this together. You have more strength and courage than you realize. Now, let's get moving. We have a Guardian Stone to find."

With Kael by her side, Liora felt a renewed sense of purpose. She still had many questions and fears, but she was no longer alone. The path ahead was uncertain and dangerous, but she was ready to embrace the adventure that awaited her. Kael turned to her, his expression serious but encouraging. "Meet me at the edge of the forest at dawn tomorrow, and bring the amulet. We must set out as soon as possible."

As Liora and Kael made their way back to Eldergrove, the weight of the amulet pressed heavily on her mind. The dark vision of the Shadow Lord and the devastation he promised haunted her thoughts. Despite Kael's reassurances, doubt gnawed at her, and fear rooted itself deep in her heart. Kael placed a comforting hand on her shoulder. "Remember, Liora, you are not alone in this. I will be by your side every step of the way. We will face the challenges together. Now, go and rest."

That evening, Liora sat alone in her room, the amulet resting on the table before her. Its soft glow seemed almost mocking, a constant reminder of the responsibility she now bore. She turned it over in her hands, the cool metal warming slightly at her touch. The memory of the vision, the Shadow Lord's burning eyes and the destruction he foretold, sent a shiver down her spine.

What if she wasn't strong enough? What if she failed, and the darkness consumed everything she loved? The burden felt too great, and she longed for the simplicity of her life before the amulet had entered it.

An idea began to form in her mind, born of desperation and fear. If she hid the amulet, if she kept it safe and out of sight, perhaps the responsibility would disappear. She could return to her life as a herbalist, tending to her plants and helping her village in the small, familiar ways she knew. Someone else, someone stronger and more capable, could take up the mantle and face the Shadow Lord.

The thought of hiding the amulet brought a strange sense of relief. She quickly packed the glowing artifact into her satchel, determination mingled with guilt. She knew it was a cowardly choice, but at that moment, it seemed the only way to escape the overwhelming burden.

Liora slipped out of her cottage, the village quiet under the cover of night. She moved silently through the familiar streets, heading toward a secluded part of the forest. Her heart pounded with each step, the night sounds of the forest amplifying her anxiety. She reached a small clearing surrounded by thick underbrush, a place she often visited when she needed solitude.

She knelt beside a large, moss-covered rock and began to dig. The soil was cool and damp beneath her fingers, the scent of earth filling her nostrils. She worked quickly, creating a small hole just large enough to conceal the amulet. With a final glance around, she placed the glowing artifact into the ground and covered it with soil and leaves.

As she stood up, a wave of relief washed over her. The amulet was hidden, the weight of its responsibility lifted from her shoulders. She took a deep breath, feeling a sense of calm she hadn't experienced since finding the artifact.

But as she turned to leave, a nagging doubt tugged at her heart. She tried to push it aside, convincing herself that someone else would find the amulet and rise to the challenge. She could return to her life, safe and undisturbed.

Back in her cottage, Liora tried to sleep, but the vision of the Shadow Lord haunted her dreams. The dark figure loomed large in her mind, his fiery eyes burning with malice. She saw the villages in ruins, the land shrouded in darkness, and the faces of her friends and family twisted in fear and despair.

She woke in a cold sweat, the remnants of the vision clinging to her like a dark cloud. She couldn't shake the feeling that she had made a terrible mistake. The amulet's glow seemed to penetrate her thoughts, a silent accusation that she had abandoned her duty.

Despite her fear, a spark of resolve ignited within her. She couldn't run from this responsibility. The vision had shown her the stakes, the danger that threatened her world. She had to find the strength within herself to face it.

As dawn broke, Liora made a decision. She would retrieve the amulet and accept the call to adventure, no matter how daunting it seemed. She couldn't let fear dictate her actions. Her village, her friends, and the entire land depended on her courage.

With renewed determination, she dressed quickly and headed back to the clearing. The morning light filtered through the trees, casting a golden glow over the forest. She reached the moss-covered rock and began to dig, her hands moving with purpose.

When she finally unearthed the amulet, its glow seemed even brighter than before, as if it recognized her renewed resolve. Liora held it tightly, feeling its warmth seep into her skin. She knew the path ahead would be difficult and fraught with danger, but she was ready to face it.

Chapter 3: The Mentor

As the first light of dawn broke over Eldergrove, the village stirred to life. Liora stood at the edge of the forest, clutching the amulet tightly. She could feel its gentle pulse, a steady reminder of the power it held and the responsibility it bestowed upon her.

Just as she began to wonder when Kael would arrive, the sound of approaching footsteps drew her attention. She turned to see the old ranger emerging from the trees, his presence as imposing and reassuring as ever. Kael's eyes immediately went to the amulet in her hand, and he nodded approvingly.

"Liora," he greeted, his voice filled with both warmth and gravity. "I see you've made your decision."

She nodded, her resolve firm. "I have. We need to find the Guardian Stone and protect it from the Shadow Lord."

Kael's expression softened into a proud smile. "Good. You have the heart of a true adventurer, Liora. But before we set out, there are things you must know."

He gestured for her to sit, and they found a spot beneath a large oak tree at the village's edge. The morning light filtered through the leaves, casting a serene glow over them. Kael settled himself on a moss-covered rock and began to speak, his voice carrying the weight of many years and many stories.

"The amulet you found is indeed the key to the Guardian Stone," Kael began. "It's said to have been created by the ancient druids, who infused it with powerful magic to protect our land from dark forces. The Guardian Stone itself is the source of this magic, a beacon of light that keeps the shadows at bay."

Liora listened intently, absorbing every word. "Have you ever seen the Guardian Stone, Kael?"

The old ranger shook his head. "No, but I've spent my life learning about it, preparing for the day it might be needed. I've traveled far and wide, seeking out knowledge and allies. The tales I've heard speak of trials and dangers that guard the Stone, tests of heart and spirit that only the worthy can overcome."

He paused, his gaze distant as if recalling memories of past adventures. "I've faced many challenges in my time, Liora. I've fought creatures born of darkness, navigated treacherous landscapes, and uncovered secrets long forgotten. But each journey has taught me something valuable, something that I can now pass on to you."

Liora felt a surge of admiration for Kael. "What can you teach me?"

Kael's eyes sparkled with a mix of wisdom and mischief. "Many things, young herbalist. You've already shown bravery and resourcefulness, but there's more to being a guardian than that. You'll need to learn how to read the land, to understand its signs and warnings. You'll need to hone your instincts, to trust your intuition even when logic fails. And most importantly, you'll need to believe in yourself and your companions."

He leaned closer, his voice dropping to a conspiratorial whisper. "Let me tell you about one of my adventures. It was many years ago, long before you were born. I was deep in the heart of the Serpent's Valley, searching for a lost relic said to grant its bearer incredible strength. The valley was a place of nightmares, filled with venomous creatures and deadly traps."

Liora's eyes widened, her imagination painting vivid pictures of Kael's tale. "What happened?"

Kael chuckled softly. "I was ambushed by a pack of shadow wolves, creatures born of pure darkness. They were fast and fierce, their eyes glowing with malevolent intent. I fought them off as best I could, but their numbers were overwhelming. Just when I thought it was the end, I remembered an old trick I'd learned from a shaman in the north. Using a special blend of herbs, I created a smoke screen that confused the wolves and allowed me to escape."

Liora leaned forward, fascinated. "What was the relic?"

Kael smiled. "Ah, the relic. It was a simple pendant, but it held a fragment of the Guardian Stone's power. Wearing it, I felt a surge of strength and clarity, enough to defeat the remaining wolves and make my way out of the valley. That pendant now resides in a safe place, waiting for the day it might be needed again."

He placed a reassuring hand on Liora's shoulder. "You see, every challenge you face will teach you something new, something that will help you on your journey. The amulet chose you because it saw your potential, your strength. Believe in that, and you will succeed."

Liora felt a wave of gratitude and determination. "Thank you, Kael. I'll do my best to learn and grow, to become the guardian this land needs."

Kael nodded, his eyes shining with pride. "I have no doubt that you will, Liora. Now, let's prepare for the journey ahead. We have much to do, and the fate of our world rests on our shoulders."

As they stood and began to make their way back to the village, Liora felt a sense of purpose and clarity. With Kael as her mentor and the amulet as her guide, she was ready to face whatever trials lay ahead. The call to adventure had been answered, and her journey was just beginning.

Kael's tales of adventure left Liora both inspired and awed. The reality of her situation settled in more deeply with every word he spoke. As they walked back to the village, Kael's demeanor grew more serious, and Liora could sense the urgency in his stride.

"Liora," Kael said, his voice firm, "the situation is more dire than you might realize. The Shadow Lord you saw in your vision is not a mere figment of your imagination. He is real, and his power grows with each passing day. If we do not act quickly, the darkness will spread, consuming everything in its path."

Liora swallowed hard, the weight of his words pressing down on her. "But why me, Kael? Why did the amulet choose me? There must be others more capable, more experienced."

Kael stopped and turned to face her, his eyes intense. "The amulet chose you because you have a rare gift, Liora. Your connection to nature, your pure heart, and your courage make you the perfect guardian. You may not see it now, but you have the strength to face this darkness. And you won't be alone. I will guide you, mentor you, and ensure you are prepared for what lies ahead."

His words stirred something deep within Liora. Despite her fears, she felt a flicker of hope and determination. "What do we need to do, Kael? How can we stop the Shadow Lord?"

Kael's expression softened, a glimmer of pride in his eyes. "We must find the Guardian Stone and awaken its full power. The stone is hidden in the heart of the Vyrn Forest, protected by ancient magic and formidable guardians. Our journey will be perilous, but with the amulet, we have a chance to succeed."

Liora nodded, her resolve strengthening. "I understand. I'm ready to do whatever it takes to protect our land."

Kael placed a reassuring hand on her shoulder. "Good. We must leave as soon as possible. Time is not on our side. I'll help you gather what you need for the journey. We'll need supplies, weapons, and knowledge of the terrain. But most importantly, you must be prepared to face your own fears and doubts."

They spent the rest of the day preparing for the journey. Kael showed Liora how to pack her satchel efficiently, ensuring they had enough provisions without being weighed down. He taught her how to sharpen her knife and use it not just as a tool but as a weapon if necessary. They studied maps of the Vyrn Forest, tracing the path they would take and noting the dangers they might encounter.

As dusk fell, Kael lit a small fire outside his cottage, and they sat together in its warm glow. He began to share more of his knowledge, teaching Liora about the different plants and creatures they might come across. He showed her how to recognize the signs of impending danger and how to use her surroundings to her advantage.

"Liora," Kael said, his tone more gentle now, "there is one more thing you must understand. This journey will test you in ways you cannot yet imagine. You will face physical challenges, yes, but the greatest battles will be within your own heart and mind. You must learn to trust yourself, to believe in your strength and your purpose. The amulet chose you because it saw something extraordinary in you. Never forget that."

Liora looked into the fire, the flames dancing and casting shadows on the ground. She felt a mixture of fear and excitement, but most of all, she felt a sense of destiny. The path ahead was uncertain and filled with danger, but with Kael by her side and the amulet in her hand, she knew she had to try.

"Thank you, Kael," she said quietly. "For believing in me. I won't let you down."

Kael smiled, a rare softness in his eyes. "I know you won't, Liora. Now, get some rest. We have a long journey ahead of us, and we'll need all our strength."

Liora nodded and made her way back to her cottage. As she lay in bed, the events of the day replayed in her mind. She felt a strange mix of exhaustion and exhilaration. The darkness she had seen in her vision still haunted her, but now, there was a light of hope, a glimmer of possibility. She drifted off to sleep, the amulet's soft glow illuminating her dreams, preparing her for the trials and triumphs that lay ahead.

The night passed slowly for Liora. Her mind raced with thoughts of the journey ahead, the dangers they would face, and the responsibility she now bore. As dawn approached, she rose from her bed with a sense of purpose and determination.

Kael was already up, preparing their supplies. He greeted her with a nod, his expression serious but encouraging. "Are you ready, Liora?"

She took a deep breath, feeling a mix of fear and excitement. "Yes, I'm ready."

Kael handed her a small, leather-bound journal. "This will be your guide and companion. Record everything you see and learn. It will help you stay focused and remember the lessons we encounter along the way."

Liora accepted the journal with a nod of gratitude. She tucked it into her satchel alongside the amulet, which now seemed to hum with a faint, reassuring warmth.

The village was quiet as they made their final preparations. A few villagers had gathered to see them off, their faces a mix of concern and hope. Among them was Mara, the village elder, who had first recognized the amulet's significance.

Mara stepped forward, her eyes filled with a mixture of pride and worry. "Liora, you are embarking on a great and perilous journey. Remember, you carry the hopes of our village with you. Stay strong and trust in your abilities."

Liora hugged Mara, feeling the elder's warmth and strength. "I will, Mara. I promise to do everything I can to protect our home."

As they moved toward the edge of the village, Liora spotted her parents standing together, their faces etched with concern. She walked over to them, taking their hands in hers.

"Be safe, Liora," her mother whispered, tears glistening in her eyes.

"You have always been strong and resourceful," her father added, his voice steady but emotional. "We believe in you."

Liora embraced them both, feeling their love and support bolster her resolve. "I'll come back. I promise."

With final farewells said, Liora and Kael set out on their journey. The path ahead was shrouded in uncertainty, but Liora felt a newfound strength within her. Kael's presence was a comforting reminder that she was not alone in this quest.

As they entered the dense forest, the sounds of the village faded, replaced by the rustling of leaves and the calls of distant birds. Kael led the way, his movements sure and confident. Liora followed closely, her senses heightened and alert.

"Remember," Kael said, his voice low but clear, "the forest can be deceptive. Trust your instincts and stay focused. We must reach the heart of Vyrn Forest as quickly as possible."

Liora nodded, her eyes scanning their surroundings. The forest was alive with magic and mystery, every shadow and sound hinting at secrets hidden within its depths.

As they walked, Kael continued to share stories of his past adventures, each tale filled with lessons and wisdom. He spoke of battles fought and won, of alliances formed with creatures of the forest, and of the strength found in moments of despair.

Liora listened intently, absorbing his words and feeling her own confidence grow. She began to see the forest not as a place of danger but as a living entity, a realm of possibilities and challenges to be faced with courage and determination.

Hours passed, the sun climbing higher in the sky. They paused briefly to rest and eat, Kael teaching Liora how to find safe, edible plants and fresh water sources. Every moment was a lesson, every step a step closer to their goal.

By late afternoon, they reached a clearing, the trees parting to reveal a tranquil glade. In the center stood a towering oak, its branches reaching skyward like ancient, gnarled fingers.

"This is our first waypoint," Kael said, his voice reverent. "The Guardian Tree. It marks the beginning of the true journey."

Liora approached the tree, feeling its ancient presence. She placed a hand on its trunk, sensing the deep-rooted strength and wisdom it held.

"We must rest here for the night," Kael continued. "The journey ahead will be even more challenging, and we need to be at our best."

As they set up camp, Liora felt a sense of calm and purpose. The weight of her destiny no longer seemed so daunting. With Kael by her side and the amulet's guidance, she was ready to face whatever lay ahead.

That night, as she lay beneath the stars, Liora reflected on the path that had brought her here. The vision of the Shadow Lord still loomed in her mind, but now it was tempered by the hope and determination she felt within herself.

She knew the journey would be long and difficult, but she was no longer afraid. She was ready to embrace her destiny, to fight for her home and her loved ones, and to uncover the secrets of the Guardian Stone.

As sleep finally claimed her, Liora dreamed not of darkness and fear, but of light and strength. The path ahead was uncertain, but she knew that with Kael's guidance and her own inner resolve, they would succeed.

Chapter 4: Crossing the Threshold

As they left the Guardian Tree behind, the path grew narrower and the forest denser. The canopy above them thickened, filtering the sunlight into a green, ethereal haze. The sounds of the forest changed, becoming more muted and mysterious. Liora felt a growing sense of anticipation and unease as they ventured deeper into the heart of the Vyrn Forest.

The Vyrn Forest was unlike any place Liora had ever known. Trees towered above them, their trunks thick with age and their leaves shimmering with a subtle, otherworldly glow. Flowers of every hue carpeted the forest floor, some emitting a soft luminescence that bathed the path in a gentle light. The air was filled with the sounds of chirping birds, rustling leaves, and the occasional distant roar of a creature Liora couldn't identify.

Kael moved with the grace and confidence of a seasoned ranger, his steps sure and silent on the forest floor. He held up a hand, signaling for Liora to pause. "We're entering a part of the forest few have ever traversed," he said, his voice low. "From here on out, we must be even more vigilant."

Liora nodded, her senses heightened and her hand resting on the hilt of her dagger. She could feel the amulet's presence, a constant reminder of their purpose and the importance of their mission.

"Be cautious, Liora," Kael warned, his eyes scanning the surroundings. "This forest is as dangerous as it is beautiful. Many creatures here are not what they seem, and the magic that flows through these woods can be both a blessing and a curse."

As they ventured deeper, the forest seemed to come alive around them. Vines moved subtly as if guided by unseen hands, and the underbrush rustled with the activity of hidden creatures. Liora's senses were on high alert, her heart pounding with both fear and excitement. She could feel the magic in the air, a palpable energy that tingled against her skin.

They came upon a clearing where a stream cut through the forest, its water sparkling with an unnatural clarity. Kael knelt by the stream, cupping his hands to drink. "This water is pure and safe," he said, gesturing for Liora to do the same. "It's one of the forest's gifts."

Liora knelt beside him, the cool water refreshing her parched throat. As she drank, she noticed small, iridescent fish darting beneath the surface, their scales catching the light in a mesmerizing display.

They continued their journey, the path growing narrower and more treacherous. Thorny brambles clawed at their clothes, and strange, flickering lights danced just out of reach. At one point, Liora stumbled upon a patch of flowers that seemed to hum with an ethereal melody, their petals vibrating in harmony with the song.

Kael paused, his expression serious. "These are Siren's Blooms. Their song can lure travelers off the path, leading them to their doom. Stay close and keep your wits about you."

Liora shivered, the flowers' haunting melody echoing in her ears as they pressed on. The forest's beauty was undeniable, but so too was its danger. Every step they took was a reminder of the delicate balance between the two.

As the hours passed, the light began to fade, casting long shadows across their path. Kael led them to a small, sheltered grove where they could rest for the night. The grove was ringed by ancient trees, their branches intertwined to form a natural canopy.

"We'll make camp here," Kael said, setting down his pack. "The forest is full of mysteries, Liora, but with each step, we grow closer to our goal. Remember the lessons you've learned today. They will serve you well in the days to come."

Liora nodded, exhaustion tugging at her limbs. As she settled down for the night, she felt a mixture of fear and determination. The forest was both magical and perilous, but with Kael by her side and the amulet guiding her, she knew she had the strength to face whatever lay ahead.

Under the shelter of the ancient trees, Liora drifted off to sleep, the sounds of the forest weaving into her dreams. The path ahead was fraught with danger, but she was ready to embrace her destiny and protect the land she loved.

As dawn broke and the forest awoke with a symphony of sounds, Liora and Kael continued their journey deeper into the Vyrn Forest. The terrain grew increasingly difficult, the path obscured by thick underbrush and twisting roots that seemed to move of their own accord. The air was thick with the scent of damp earth and the sweet aroma of wildflowers, a mixture both comforting and unsettling.

"Stay close, Liora," Kael instructed, his voice low and steady. "The deeper we go, the more the forest will test us."

Liora nodded, her senses heightened and alert. Every rustle in the leaves, every shadow flickering at the corner of her vision, made her heart race. She could feel the amulet's reassuring weight against her chest, its gentle pulse a reminder of her purpose.

Their first challenge came in the form of a dense thicket of brambles, their thorny vines twisting and writhing as if alive. Kael took out a small, serrated knife and began to carefully cut a path through the vegetation, motioning for Liora to follow closely behind.

"These are Shadow Thorns," Kael explained, his voice tense. "Their vines can ensnare you if you're not careful. Move quickly but carefully."

Liora followed his lead, mimicking his precise movements as they navigated through the brambles. She felt a vine brush against her arm and quickly pulled away, narrowly avoiding its grasp. Her heart pounded, but she kept her focus, her trust in Kael growing with each step.

As they emerged from the thicket, Liora felt a rush of relief, only to be confronted by their next challenge. The ground before them shimmered with an iridescent sheen, the air around it buzzing with an unnatural energy.

"This is an Enchanted Mire," Kael said, studying the terrain. "It's treacherous, but if we move carefully, we can get through. Follow my lead and step where I step."

Liora watched intently as Kael moved forward, his steps deliberate and precise. She mirrored his actions, feeling the ground shift beneath her feet. The air crackled with magic, and she had to fight to maintain her balance.

Halfway through the mire, Liora's foot slipped, and she felt herself sinking into the soft, enchanted earth. Panic surged through her, but Kael was there in an instant, his strong hand pulling her back to solid ground.

"Trust your instincts, Liora," he reminded her, his eyes steady and reassuring. "You have the strength to overcome these challenges."

She nodded, taking a deep breath to steady herself. With Kael's guidance, they made it through the Enchanted Mire, emerging onto firmer ground. Liora felt a sense of accomplishment, her confidence growing with each obstacle they overcame.

Their next challenge came in the form of a clearing filled with strange, luminescent plants. The air was thick with their sweet, cloying scent, and Liora noticed the remains of small animals scattered around the base of the plants.

"These are Carnivorous Blooms," Kael warned, his voice grim. "Their beauty hides their danger. Stay close and do not touch the flowers."

As they carefully navigated the clearing, Liora's senses were on high alert. She could see the delicate, almost hypnotic movement of the blooms as they swayed gently in the breeze, their luminescence casting eerie shadows. The air seemed to hum with a quiet menace, and she felt a chill run down her spine.

Just as they were about to leave the clearing, Liora spotted a small, glowing herb nestled among the deadly blooms. Its faint light was different from the others, and she recognized it from her studies—Moonshade, a rare and powerful healing plant.

"Kael, look," she whispered, pointing to the herb. "It's Moonshade. It could be incredibly useful."

Kael glanced at the plant, his expression thoughtful. "It's risky, but if you think you can get it safely, it might be worth it."

Liora nodded, her determination outweighing her fear. She carefully edged closer to the Moonshade, her movements slow and deliberate. She could feel the eyes of the Carnivorous Blooms on her, their petals quivering as if sensing her presence. With a swift but gentle motion, she plucked the Moonshade and quickly retreated, the blooms rustling ominously behind her.

Kael smiled, a glimmer of pride in his eyes. "Well done, Liora. You trusted your instincts and succeeded."

Liora felt a surge of pride and relief. Each challenge they faced strengthened her resolve and deepened her trust in Kael. She began to understand the forest's language, its subtle signs and warnings, and she felt a growing connection to the magical world around her.

As they continued their journey, Liora's confidence blossomed. The path ahead was fraught with danger, but she knew she was not alone. With Kael's guidance and her own growing strength, she felt ready to face whatever lay ahead. The journey was just beginning, and she was determined to see it through, to protect her village and the land she loved.

As the sun dipped below the horizon, casting the forest in shades of twilight, an eerie stillness settled over the Vyrn Forest. Liora and Kael made their way through a dense grove, the ancient trees looming overhead, their branches intertwining like skeletal fingers. The path ahead was shrouded in darkness, the fading light barely penetrating the thick canopy.

"We should find a place to camp soon," Kael said, his voice barely a whisper in the growing gloom. "The forest is more dangerous at night."

Liora nodded, her senses alert. The events of the day had left her exhausted, but her determination remained unwavering. They continued walking, the forest growing quieter with each passing moment. The usual sounds of nocturnal creatures were absent, replaced by an oppressive silence that made Liora's skin prickle with unease.

Suddenly, a low growl echoed through the trees, followed by another and then another. Liora froze, her heart pounding. She turned to Kael, whose face was set in grim determination.

"Shadow Wolves," he murmured, drawing his sword. "Servants of the dark force. Stay close and be ready to defend yourself."

Liora's breath caught in her throat as she unsheathed the small dagger Kael had given her. She had trained with it briefly, but this was different. This was real danger, and her hands trembled with fear and anticipation.

The first wolf emerged from the shadows, its eyes glowing a malevolent red. Its sleek, black fur seemed to absorb the light, and its snarl revealed rows of sharp, glistening teeth. More wolves followed, surrounding them in a semi-circle, their growls growing louder and more menacing.

Kael stepped forward, his sword gleaming in the dim light. "Back, creatures!" he shouted, his voice strong and commanding. "We mean you no harm, but we will defend ourselves."

The wolves snarled in response, inching closer. Liora's grip tightened on her dagger, her heart racing. She could feel the amulet's pulse quicken, as if reacting to the danger around them.

With a sudden, coordinated movement, the wolves attacked. Kael moved with the grace and speed of a seasoned warrior, his sword slicing through the air in a blur of steel. He struck down the first wolf that lunged at him, its body dissolving into shadows as it fell.

Liora fought to keep her fear at bay, her mind racing. She remembered Kael's lessons, the importance of trusting her instincts. As a wolf lunged at her, she sidestepped and slashed with her dagger, the blade grazing its flank. The wolf yelped and retreated, its eyes burning with fury.

Kael was a whirlwind of motion, fending off multiple wolves with skill and precision. Liora felt a surge of adrenaline as she parried another attack, her movements becoming more fluid and confident. She and Kael moved in tandem, their actions synchronized in a deadly dance of survival.

Despite their efforts, the wolves continued to press in, their numbers seemingly endless. Liora's arms ached, and her breaths came in ragged gasps, but she refused to give up. She glanced at Kael, who fought with unwavering resolve, his presence a steady anchor amidst the chaos.

Suddenly, a particularly large wolf lunged at Liora, its teeth bared and eyes blazing. She stumbled, her dagger slipping from her grasp. Time seemed to slow as the wolf bore down on her, its maw opening wide.

But Kael was there, his sword striking with deadly precision. The wolf yelped and collapsed, dissolving into shadows like the others. Kael helped Liora to her feet, his grip firm and reassuring.

"We need to get out of here," he said urgently, his eyes scanning the dark forest. "There are too many of them."

Liora nodded, her fear giving way to determination. Together, they fought their way through the remaining wolves, their path illuminated by the faint glow of the amulet. The forest seemed to close in around them, the shadows thick and oppressive, but they pressed on, refusing to yield.

Finally, they broke through the line of wolves, their bodies slick with sweat and their breaths heavy. The wolves, sensing their retreat, did not pursue, their growls fading into the distance.

Kael and Liora stumbled into a small clearing, their bodies aching from the battle. They collapsed onto the ground, the adrenaline slowly ebbing away. Liora's hands trembled as she retrieved her dagger, her mind racing with the events of the night.

Kael placed a reassuring hand on her shoulder. "You did well, Liora. You fought bravely."

Liora nodded, her heart still pounding. "I couldn't have done it without you, Kael. Thank you."

Their eyes met, and in that moment, a bond was forged. They had faced their first real danger together and emerged stronger for it. The challenges ahead were daunting, but they knew they could rely on each other.

As they rested in the clearing, the sounds of the forest slowly returned, a reminder of the world they were fighting to protect. Liora felt a renewed sense of purpose, her fear tempered by the knowledge that she was not alone.

With Kael by her side and the amulet guiding them, she was ready to face whatever dangers lay ahead. Their journey was just beginning, and together, they would find the Guardian Stone and repel the darkness threatening their land.

Chapter 5: Tests, Allies, and Enemies

The morning sun filtered through the dense canopy of the Vyrn Forest, casting dappled light on the forest floor as Liora and Kael resumed their journey. The battle with the shadow wolves had left them both weary, but their resolve was stronger than ever. They pressed onward, the weight of their mission heavy but their determination unshaken.

The forest seemed to sense their purpose, its mystical energy palpable with every step they took. As they ventured deeper, the trees grew taller and more ancient, their bark etched with strange, intricate patterns. The air was thick with magic, and Liora could feel its presence tingling against her skin.

"Stay alert," Kael advised, his eyes scanning the surroundings. "The deeper we go, the more the forest will test us. Trust your instincts and remember what you've learned."

Liora nodded, her grip tightening on her satchel. The amulet's steady pulse provided a constant reminder of their mission. She felt a growing connection to the forest, its magic resonating with the power of the amulet.

Their next trial came in the form of a towering stone archway, covered in ancient runes that glowed faintly in the dim light. The archway blocked their path, and the runes seemed to shift and change as they approached, forming an impenetrable barrier.

Liora stepped closer, her eyes narrowing as she studied the runes. She recognized some of the symbols from her grandmother's stories, tales of ancient magic and forgotten knowledge. She reached out, her fingers brushing against the cool stone, and felt a surge of energy flow through her.

"These runes are a test," she murmured, turning to Kael. "We need to decipher them to pass through."

Kael nodded, his expression serious. "What do they say?"

Liora focused on the runes, her mind racing as she tried to recall the lessons her grandmother had taught her. The symbols seemed to dance before her eyes, their meanings just out of reach. She took a deep breath, closing her eyes and letting the magic of the forest guide her.

Slowly, the runes began to make sense. She traced their patterns with her finger, murmuring the words aloud as she deciphered them. "Strength in unity, courage in adversity, wisdom in humility. These are the keys to passage."

Kael watched her, his eyes filled with respect. "You're doing well, Liora. Keep going."

Encouraged by his words, Liora continued to decipher the runes. She felt the barrier begin to weaken, the energy around them shifting as she spoke the final words. With a soft, resonant hum, the archway's runes faded, and the barrier dissolved.

"We did it," Liora said, a mixture of relief and pride in her voice.

Kael smiled, his eyes shining with approval. "You did it, Liora. Your knowledge and courage are guiding us."

They stepped through the archway, the path ahead revealing itself once more. The forest grew darker and more foreboding, but Liora felt a renewed sense of purpose. The trials were not just obstacles but lessons, each one teaching her something new about herself and her abilities.

Their next trial came in the form of a narrow ravine, its rocky walls covered in a thick, slippery moss. A fast-flowing river roared at the bottom, the water frothing and churning with dangerous currents. The only way across was a series of precarious stepping stones, each one slick with moisture.

Kael tested the first stone with his foot, then glanced back at Liora. "We'll have to move quickly and carefully. One slip, and we're in trouble."

Liora nodded, her heart pounding as she stared at the treacherous path. She took a deep breath, focusing on the amulet's steady pulse, and followed Kael onto the first stone. The rock shifted slightly under her weight, and she had to fight to keep her balance.

Kael moved with the grace of a seasoned ranger, his steps sure and confident. Liora mirrored his movements, her instincts guiding her as she leaped from stone to stone. The roar of the river filled her ears, the cold spray of the water chilling her skin, but she pressed on, her fear tempered by determination.

Halfway across, Liora's foot slipped on a particularly slick stone. She gasped, her arms flailing for balance, and felt herself teetering on the edge. Kael was there in an instant, his strong hand gripping hers and pulling her back to safety.

"Stay focused," he urged, his eyes locked on hers. "You can do this."

Liora nodded, her breath coming in ragged gasps. She steadied herself, her resolve hardening, and continued across the remaining stones. Each leap felt like a test of her courage, but with Kael's support and her own growing confidence, she made it to the other side.

They collapsed onto the rocky shore, their breaths heavy with exertion. Liora's muscles ached, but a sense of accomplishment washed over her. She had faced her fears and emerged stronger.

Kael looked at her, his expression one of admiration. "You're growing, Liora. Each trial is making you stronger, more capable."

Liora smiled, feeling a warmth in her chest. "Thank you, Kael. I couldn't do this without you."

As they rested, the forest around them seemed to hum with approval, its magic resonating with their shared determination. The path ahead was fraught with trials, but Liora knew that with Kael's guidance and her own inner strength, they would overcome them together.

As the sun climbed higher, casting a warm glow over the forest, Liora and Kael continued their journey. The trials they had faced had strengthened their resolve, but the path ahead was still uncertain. They walked in companionable silence, each lost in their thoughts, when the sound of rustling leaves and snapping branches broke the tranquility.

Kael drew his sword, and Liora tensed, her hand hovering over her dagger. From the underbrush emerged a tall, imposing figure, his dark eyes scanning the surroundings with a wary intensity. His clothes were rugged, his armor scratched and dented, and a massive sword was slung across his back. He moved with the grace of a predator, his every step calculated and deliberate.

Kael stepped forward, his stance defensive. "Who are you?" he demanded, his voice steady.

The stranger raised his hands in a gesture of peace. "I mean no harm," he said, his voice deep and resonant. "My name is Aric. I've been following the signs, drawn by the same force that brought you here."

Liora studied him, her curiosity piqued. There was something enigmatic about Aric, a darkness that seemed to cling to him, but also a sense of strength and purpose.

Kael eyed Aric warily but lowered his sword slightly. "Why are you here?"

Aric met Kael's gaze, his expression unreadable. "I seek the Guardian Stone. The dark force threatens us all, and I believe our paths are intertwined."

Before Kael could respond, a soft, melodic voice interrupted. "He speaks the truth."

From the shadows of the trees stepped a woman, her presence almost ethereal. She wore flowing robes adorned with intricate symbols, and a staff of polished wood rested in her hand. Her eyes, a striking shade of violet, shimmered with an otherworldly light.

"I am Elara," she said, inclining her head in greeting. "A mage of the Silver Crescent. I have sensed the awakening of the amulet and the darkness that follows. We must work together if we are to succeed."

Liora felt a surge of hope and relief. The arrival of Aric and Elara, each bringing unique skills, seemed like a sign from the forest itself. She glanced at Kael, who gave a small nod, his expression thoughtful.

"Very well," Kael said, sheathing his sword. "We can use all the help we can get. But know this: our mission is dangerous, and trust must be earned."

Aric nodded, his face solemn. "I understand. My past is my own, but I swear my loyalty to our cause."

Elara stepped forward, her violet eyes meeting Liora's. "You carry the amulet, the key to finding the Guardian Stone. Its magic is ancient and powerful. I will aid you in unlocking its secrets."

Liora felt a warmth spread through her chest, the weight of her responsibility lightened by the presence of her new allies. "Thank you," she said, her voice steady. "Together, we can face whatever trials lie ahead."

As they set off once more, the forest seemed to shift around them, its energy welcoming the new additions to their group. The path was no less perilous, but with Aric's strength and Elara's wisdom, Liora felt more confident in their ability to succeed.

Their first test as a team came swiftly. As they approached a narrow ravine, similar to the one they had crossed earlier, the ground began to tremble. Liora felt the amulet pulse urgently, a warning of impending danger.

"Stay close," Kael ordered, his eyes scanning the surroundings.

From the shadows emerged creatures unlike any Liora had seen before. They were humanoid, with leathery wings and claws that gleamed in the dim light. Their eyes glowed with a malevolent red, similar to the shadow wolves, and they moved with eerie coordination.

Aric drew his sword, his expression grim. "Winged Reapers," he muttered. "Servants of the dark force."

Elara stepped forward, her staff glowing with a soft, white light. "Prepare yourselves. These creatures are relentless."

The Reapers attacked with a ferocity that took Liora's breath away. Kael and Aric fought side by side, their swords flashing as they parried and struck. Elara chanted incantations, her staff emitting bursts of magical energy that repelled the attackers.

Liora, heart pounding, focused on the amulet's pulse. She felt its magic intertwining with her own, guiding her actions. With a swift motion, she drew her dagger and moved to assist her companions, her fear tempered by determination.

One of the Reapers lunged at her, its claws outstretched. Liora sidestepped, her dagger slicing through the creature's wing. It shrieked and fell back, its body dissolving into shadows.

Kael fought with precision and strength, his movements a blur of controlled power. Aric, despite his brooding demeanor, fought with a fierce intensity, his sword cleaving through the Reapers with deadly accuracy. Elara's magic provided a shield, her spells warding off the brunt of the attack.

As the battle raged, Liora found herself relying on her instincts and the lessons she had learned. She moved with confidence, her attacks more precise, her fear giving way to a growing sense of unity with her companions.

Finally, the last of the Reapers fell, its body disintegrating into shadowy mist. The forest grew silent once more, the only sound their heavy breathing and the rustling of leaves in the wind.

Kael sheathed his sword, his eyes meeting Liora's. "Well done, everyone. We fought as one, and we emerged victorious."

Aric nodded, his expression softening. "We make a formidable team."

Elara smiled, her violet eyes glowing with approval. "Indeed. Our combined strength and skills will be crucial in the trials to come."

Liora felt a surge of pride and camaraderie. Despite their different backgrounds and the secrets they each carried, they had come together as a team. The path ahead was still fraught with danger, but they were no longer alone.

As they continued their journey, the bond between them grew stronger. Liora felt a renewed sense of hope, her heart buoyed by the presence of her allies. With Kael's guidance, Aric's strength, and Elara's wisdom, she knew they could face any challenge the forest—and the dark force—threw their way.

As the sun dipped lower in the sky, casting long shadows through the ancient trees, the forest seemed to grow more foreboding. The air was thick with the scent of pine and moss, but also something darker, an undercurrent of malevolence that set Liora on edge. She glanced at her companions, drawing strength from their presence. Together, they pressed onward, ever vigilant.

Their path wound through a dense thicket, the underbrush rustling with unseen creatures. Suddenly, a chilling howl pierced the air, followed by a chorus of guttural snarls. The group halted, weapons drawn, their eyes scanning the shadows.

Kael's voice was low and urgent. "Malakar's minions. They must be close. Stay alert and move quietly."

They continued cautiously, every step deliberate and silent. The forest seemed to close in around them, the trees forming a labyrinth of shadows and hidden threats. Liora's heart pounded in her chest, the amulet's pulse a steady reminder of the danger they faced.

As they neared a small clearing, they heard voices—harsh and guttural, speaking in a language Liora couldn't understand. Kael motioned for them to stop and crouched low, peering through the foliage.

In the clearing, a group of dark-clad figures stood around a makeshift camp. Their eyes glowed with an unnatural light, and their movements were quick and jerky, as if driven by some unseen force. At their center was a tall, imposing figure clad in black armor, a cruel smile playing on his lips.

"Malakar's minions," Kael whispered, his grip tightening on his sword. "They're searching for the Guardian Stone too. We can't let them find it."

Liora's heart raced. The sight of the enemy so close, their dark energy palpable, filled her with dread. She glanced at her companions, seeing the same determination mirrored in their eyes.

"We need a plan," Aric said, his voice a low growl. "We can't take them all on at once."

Elara nodded, her eyes narrowing in thought. "I can create a diversion, draw some of them away. Kael and Aric, you take out the sentries. Liora and I will disable their leader."

Kael nodded, his eyes flashing with approval. "Good plan. Stay close and watch each other's backs."

Elara raised her staff, murmuring an incantation. A soft, shimmering light enveloped her, and she stepped into the clearing, her presence suddenly amplified by a blinding flash. The minions recoiled, shielding their eyes from the burst of magic.

"Now!" Kael hissed, and he and Aric sprang into action. They moved with silent efficiency, their blades slicing through the air as they took down the sentries one by one. The dark-clad figures fell with barely a sound, their bodies dissolving into shadow.

Liora and Elara advanced toward the leader, who had recovered from the initial shock and now glared at them with malevolent fury. He drew a wicked-looking sword, its blade crackling with dark energy.

"You will not stop us," he snarled, lunging at them with terrifying speed.

Elara raised her staff, conjuring a shield of shimmering light that deflected his blow. Liora felt the amulet's pulse quicken, its magic flowing through her. She focused, drawing on the amulet's power, and stepped forward, her dagger ready.

The leader's eyes locked onto hers, and he sneered. "You think a mere girl can defeat me?"

Liora's fear melted away, replaced by a fierce determination. "I'm not just a girl," she said, her voice steady. "I'm the guardian of the amulet, and I will protect the Guardian Stone."

With a swift, fluid motion, she dodged his next attack and struck with her dagger. The blade, imbued with the amulet's magic, glowed with a bright, white light. It sliced through the leader's armor, and he howled in pain, dark energy spilling from the wound.

Elara seized the moment, chanting a spell that bound the leader in chains of light. He struggled, his movements growing weaker as the magic sapped his strength.

Kael and Aric joined them, their faces grim but victorious. "We need to move," Kael said urgently. "More of Malakar's minions will be coming."

They hurried away from the clearing, the sounds of the forest returning to normal as they put distance between themselves and the enemy camp. Liora's heart still pounded, but a sense of accomplishment buoyed her spirits. They had faced Malakar's minions and emerged victorious, their bond as a team stronger than ever.

As night fell, they found a sheltered grove and made camp. The flickering firelight cast dancing shadows on the trees, and Liora felt a moment of peace. They were one step closer to finding the Guardian Stone and protecting their land from the encroaching darkness.

Elara sat beside her, her violet eyes soft with understanding. "You did well today, Liora. Your courage and the power of the amulet are formidable."

Liora smiled, feeling a warmth spread through her chest. "Thank you, Elara. I couldn't have done it without all of you."

Kael and Aric joined them, their expressions weary but satisfied. "We've faced our first real test as a team," Kael said, his voice filled with quiet pride. "And we've proven we can handle whatever comes our way."

Aric nodded, his dark eyes glinting in the firelight. "There will be more challenges, more enemies. But together, we can overcome them."

Liora looked around at her companions, feeling a deep sense of gratitude and unity. They were more than just allies; they were a team, bound by a common purpose and a shared determination to protect their world.

As the stars twinkled above and the fire crackled softly, Liora felt a renewed sense of hope. The journey was far from over, and the path ahead was fraught with danger, but she knew they were ready to face it—together.

Chapter 6: Approach to the Inmost Cave

The days that followed their encounter with Malakar's minions were filled with tense anticipation and cautious progress. Each step brought Liora, Kael, Aric, and Elara closer to their goal—the hidden sanctuary where the Guardian Stone was kept. The forest seemed to grow more mystical and ancient with every mile, the air thick with magic and secrets.

Finally, after what felt like an eternity of navigating treacherous terrain and fending off lurking dangers, they stood before a towering cliff face. The entrance to the sanctuary was hidden in the rock, concealed by a shimmering veil of enchantment that pulsed with an ethereal glow.

Liora felt a shiver of awe and trepidation as she approached the barrier. The amulet thrummed against her chest, its magic resonating with the protective spell.

"This is it," Kael said, his voice hushed with reverence. "The entrance to the hidden sanctuary."

Elara stepped forward, her eyes scanning the intricate patterns that danced across the veil. "The enchantment is ancient and powerful. We must solve the puzzle to gain entry."

Liora examined the shimmering barrier, her mind racing. She could see faint symbols and runes woven into the enchantment, each one shifting and changing as she watched. It was like a living puzzle, its solution hidden within its ever-changing patterns.

"We need to decipher these runes," Liora said, her voice steady despite the challenge before them. "It's a test of our knowledge and our connection to the magic of the forest."

Aric stood guard, his hand on the hilt of his sword, his eyes scanning the surrounding area for any sign of danger. "I'll keep watch. You three focus on the puzzle."

Kael and Elara joined Liora at the barrier, their eyes studying the runes. Kael's experience and Elara's magical knowledge were invaluable, and together they began to piece together the meaning of the symbols.

"The runes speak of balance," Kael said, his brow furrowed in concentration. "Light and shadow, life and death. It's a reflection of the dual nature of the forest."

Elara nodded, her fingers tracing the shifting patterns. "We must align the runes to restore balance. Each symbol has a counterpart that completes it."

Liora focused on the runes, her mind attuning to their rhythm. She could feel the amulet's power guiding her, its magic intertwining with her own. She reached out, her fingers brushing against the shimmering surface, and the runes responded, shifting and aligning under her touch.

"Here," she said, her voice filled with certainty. "This rune represents life, and its counterpart is death. We need to bring them together."

Kael and Elara followed her lead, their combined efforts bringing the runes into alignment. The barrier began to pulse more rapidly, the patterns merging and solidifying.

As they worked, the air around them seemed to hum with anticipation. Liora's heart pounded in her chest, each successful alignment bringing them closer to their goal. She could feel the sanctuary's magic responding, recognizing their efforts and granting them access.

Finally, with a soft, resonant hum, the runes locked into place. The barrier shimmered brightly and then dissolved, revealing a dark, narrow passage leading into the heart of the cliff.

"We did it," Liora breathed, her voice filled with awe and relief.

Kael placed a hand on her shoulder, his eyes shining with pride. "Well done, Liora. Your intuition and courage have brought us this far."

Elara smiled, her violet eyes glowing with approval. "The sanctuary awaits. We must proceed with caution. The trials within will be even more challenging."

Aric joined them, his gaze steady and resolute. "We're ready. Whatever lies ahead, we'll face it together."

With a shared sense of determination, they stepped into the passage, the air growing cooler and the light dimming as they ventured deeper into the cliff. The walls of the tunnel were adorned with ancient carvings, their meanings lost to time but their beauty undiminished.

As they moved forward, the tunnel widened into a vast cavern, its ceiling lost in darkness. The faint glow of bioluminescent fungi cast an eerie light, illuminating the path ahead.

Liora felt a surge of anticipation. The Guardian Stone was close, and with it, the power to repel the darkness threatening their land. But she knew the trials were far from over. They had entered the sanctuary, but the true test of their courage, wisdom, and unity lay ahead.

Together, they pressed on, their hearts filled with hope and determination. The journey was far from over, but they were ready to face whatever challenges awaited them in the inmost cave.

As they ventured deeper into the cavern, the air grew colder, and the darkness pressed in around them. The bioluminescent fungi provided a faint, eerie light, casting long shadows that danced on the ancient stone walls. Liora's heart pounded in her chest, a mixture of fear and anticipation churning within her. The reality of their journey, the weight of their mission, bore down on her like never before.

Every step they took echoed through the cavern, a haunting reminder of the solitude and danger that lay ahead. Liora's mind raced with doubts and fears. What if she wasn't strong enough? What if she failed and the darkness consumed their world? She felt a gnawing uncertainty, a voice in her mind whispering that she was not the hero they needed.

Kael noticed her hesitation and placed a comforting hand on her shoulder. His touch was steady, his gaze reassuring. "Liora, you've come this far. You've faced every challenge with courage and determination. Trust in yourself and in the strength of our group."

Liora met his eyes, finding solace in his confidence. "But what if I make a mistake? What if I lead us into danger?"

Kael smiled gently. "We all have doubts, Liora. Even the greatest heroes faced moments of fear and uncertainty. It's how we overcome them that defines us. You are not alone. We are in this together."

Aric stepped forward, his dark eyes intense but kind. "Kael is right. You've shown remarkable courage and wisdom. You've led us through trials that many would have faltered in. Trust in your instincts. We believe in you."

Elara nodded, her violet eyes glowing softly in the dim light. "Liora, you possess a rare gift. The amulet chose you because it sensed your potential. We are here to support you, to stand by your side. Together, we are stronger than any challenge we face."

Liora took a deep breath, feeling the warmth of their words and the strength of their conviction. Her doubts didn't vanish, but they no longer felt insurmountable. She wasn't alone. She had allies, friends who believed in her even when she doubted herself.

"Thank you," she said, her voice steady. "I'll do my best. Let's continue."

With renewed determination, they pressed onward, the path ahead growing more treacherous. The air grew colder, and the darkness deepened, but Liora felt a spark of hope rekindled within her. She focused on the amulet's pulse, its warmth a constant reminder of the magic and responsibility she carried.

The cavern walls began to close in, the passage narrowing until they had to move single file. The ground beneath them was uneven, strewn with loose rocks and hidden pitfalls. Liora led the way, her senses attuned to every sound and movement.

As they navigated a particularly narrow section, the floor beneath them suddenly gave way. Liora gasped as she tumbled into the darkness, her heart racing. She reached out, her fingers scrabbling for purchase on the slick stone walls.

Kael was there in an instant, his strong hand gripping hers and pulling her to safety. "Careful," he said, his voice calm but urgent. "The path is fraught with hidden dangers. We must tread carefully."

Liora nodded, her heart still pounding from the close call. "Thank you, Kael. I'll be more cautious."

They continued, the passage finally opening into a vast chamber. The ceiling was lost in shadow, and the air was thick with an ancient, powerful magic. At the center of the chamber stood a massive stone door, covered in intricate carvings and glowing runes.

"This is it," Elara whispered, her voice filled with awe. "The final barrier to the Guardian Stone."

Liora approached the door, her eyes scanning the runes. She could feel the amulet's energy resonating with the magic of the door, guiding her. The carvings depicted scenes of light and darkness, of battles fought and won, and of a powerful stone at the heart of it all.

"We need to decipher the runes to unlock the door," Liora said, her voice steady despite the enormity of the task.

Kael, Aric, and Elara joined her, their combined knowledge and skills focused on the puzzle before them. Liora felt a surge of confidence, her doubts overshadowed by the strength of their unity. Together, they began to decipher the runes, their minds and hearts working in harmony.

Each symbol unlocked a part of the story, revealing the secrets of the Guardian Stone and the trials it had faced throughout the ages. The runes spoke of sacrifice and courage, of the eternal struggle between light and darkness, and of the power of unity and belief.

As they worked, the door began to glow brighter, the carvings shifting and aligning. Liora felt the amulet's pulse quicken, its energy merging with the magic of the door. With a final, resonant hum, the door unlocked, swinging open to reveal the sanctum beyond.

They stepped into the sanctum, the air thick with an ancient, powerful magic. At the center of the room stood the Guardian Stone, its surface shimmering with an ethereal light. Liora felt a sense of awe and reverence, the weight of their journey and the importance of their mission crystallizing in that moment.

"You did it, Liora," Kael said, his voice filled with pride. "You led us here."

Liora nodded, her eyes fixed on the Guardian Stone. "We did it. Together."

The trials were far from over, but with her friends by her side and the power of the Guardian Stone within reach, Liora felt ready to face whatever challenges lay ahead. They had come this far, and together, they would protect their world from the darkness that threatened to consume it.

The sanctum's air was charged with a palpable sense of ancient power, the Guardian Stone at its center radiating a soft, mesmerizing glow. Liora and her companions stood at the threshold, the weight of their journey and the trials they had faced mingling with the anticipation of the challenges yet to come.

"We've made it this far," Kael said, his voice steady and resolute. "But the true test lies ahead. The sanctuary will protect the Guardian Stone with everything it has. We must be prepared."

Liora nodded, her eyes fixed on the stone. It seemed almost alive, its light pulsing in rhythm with her heartbeat. The amulet around her neck thrummed in response, its energy intertwining with that of the Guardian Stone. She felt a surge of determination, the support of her friends bolstering her resolve.

Elara stepped forward, her staff glowing faintly. "The sanctuary's magic is powerful and ancient. It will test our strength, our wisdom, and our unity. We must face these trials together."

Aric drew his sword, his expression fierce and unwavering. "Whatever comes, we'll face it head-on. We've proven we can handle anything the forest throws at us."

Liora took a deep breath, feeling the weight of the amulet and the responsibility it represented. She looked at each of her companions, drawing strength from their confidence and resolve. "Let's do this," she said, her voice firm. "Together."

They moved deeper into the sanctum, the light of the Guardian Stone casting long shadows on the walls. The air grew colder, and the sense of magic intensified, wrapping around them like a tangible force. As they approached the stone, the ground beneath them began to tremble, and the carvings on the walls seemed to come to life, shifting and changing before their eyes.

"The first trial is upon us," Elara said, her voice echoing through the chamber. "Be ready."

A deep rumble filled the air, and the ground shook violently. From the shadows emerged spectral figures, their forms flickering with an otherworldly light. They moved with a haunting grace, their eyes glowing with an eerie, unnatural fire.

"Spectral Guardians," Kael muttered, his grip tightening on his sword. "They protect the sanctum from intruders. We must prove our worth."

The Spectral Guardians advanced, their movements fluid and silent. Liora felt a chill run down her spine, but she stood her ground, the amulet's warmth a reassuring presence. She raised her dagger, its blade glowing with the same light as the amulet.

Kael and Aric moved to intercept the guardians, their swords flashing in the dim light. Elara chanted an incantation, her staff emitting a pulse of energy that pushed the specters back. The room was filled with the clash of metal and the crackle of magic, the air thick with tension.

Liora focused on the amulet, drawing on its power. She could feel its energy flowing through her, merging with her own. She stepped forward, her movements guided by instinct and the amulet's magic. With a swift motion, she struck at one of the Spectral Guardians, her blade cutting through its ethereal form. The guardian let out a haunting wail and dissolved into mist.

"Keep fighting!" Kael shouted, his sword cleaving through another guardian. "We can do this!"

Liora's confidence grew with each successful strike. She moved with a newfound grace, her fear giving way to determination. The Spectral Guardians were relentless, but with Kael, Aric, and Elara by her side, she felt unstoppable.

One by one, the guardians fell, their forms dissipating into the air. The ground stopped shaking, and the carvings on the walls stilled, the chamber returning to its previous state. The light of the Guardian Stone pulsed more brightly, as if acknowledging their victory.

"We did it," Aric said, his breath coming in heavy gasps. "The first trial is over."

Elara lowered her staff, her eyes glowing with pride. "We've proven our worth. But there will be more challenges ahead."

Kael sheathed his sword, his face serious but determined. "We've faced the Spectral Guardians. Now, we must be ready for whatever comes next."

Liora nodded, her heart still racing but filled with a sense of accomplishment. "We'll face it together," she said, her voice strong. "No matter what comes, we'll protect the Guardian Stone."

As they regrouped, the light of the Guardian Stone bathed them in its gentle glow, a reminder of the power they sought to protect. The trials had only just begun, but with their combined strength and unity, Liora knew they could overcome anything.

The path ahead was fraught with danger, but they were ready. Together, they would face the challenges of the sanctuary, protect the Guardian Stone, and repel the darkness threatening their land. Their journey was far from over, but with each step, they grew stronger and more determined, united in their quest to save their world.

Chapter 7: The Ordeal

As they entered the inner chamber of the sanctuary, the atmosphere grew heavy with a palpable sense of ancient magic. The walls were lined with intricate carvings that seemed to move and shift when viewed from the corner of the eye. The air was cool, tinged with the scent of old stone and faint traces of incense. A soft, ethereal glow emanated from crystals embedded in the walls, casting shifting patterns of light and shadow.

Liora's heart pounded in her chest, each step echoing in the stillness. Her thoughts raced, filled with a mixture of awe and apprehension. She glanced at Kael, who walked beside her with a calm, focused expression, his eyes scanning their surroundings for any sign of danger.

"This place feels... alive," Liora whispered, her voice barely more than a breath.

Kael nodded, his gaze unwavering. "The sanctuary has a will of its own. It will test us, but we must remain vigilant and work together."

Aric tightened his grip on his sword, his eyes flickering with determination. "Stay sharp. These traps will be unlike anything we've faced before."

Elara raised her staff, its light casting protective shadows around them. "We must be prepared for anything. The magic here is powerful and unpredictable."

The first challenge came quickly. As they stepped forward, the floor beneath them shifted, revealing a series of pressure plates. Liora felt her breath catch as she noticed the intricate pattern of runes etched into the stone, each one glowing faintly.

"We need to figure out the correct sequence," Elara said, studying the runes. "One wrong step, and the trap will be triggered."

Liora focused on the runes, her mind racing as she tried to decipher their meaning. She could feel the amulet's warmth against her chest, its magic guiding her thoughts. "It's a pattern of balance," she murmured. "Light and shadow, fire and water. We need to step on the symbols in pairs."

Kael nodded, his eyes meeting hers with a reassuring glance. "We trust you, Liora. Lead the way."

Taking a deep breath, Liora stepped forward, carefully placing her foot on a rune representing fire. Kael followed, stepping on the corresponding water symbol. One by one, they navigated the pressure plates, each successful step filling Liora with a growing sense of confidence.

Just as they reached the end of the trap, a sudden tremor shook the ground. Liora's eyes widened in alarm as the walls began to close in, their surfaces bristling with sharp spikes.

"Run!" Kael shouted, his voice echoing through the chamber.

They sprinted forward, the walls closing in behind them. Liora's heart raced, her mind a blur of panic and determination. She could hear the others' footsteps pounding beside her, their breaths ragged with exertion.

In the chaos, Liora tripped over a loose stone, her body slamming into the cold floor. She heard Kael's voice calling her name, but the noise was drowned out by the grinding of stone as the walls continued to close in.

A sudden force pulled her away from the group, a powerful magical current that swept her through a hidden passage. The world spun around her, a whirlwind of light and shadow, until she landed in a separate chamber, the passage sealing behind her with a resonant thud.

Disoriented and alone, Liora struggled to her feet, her heart pounding with fear and uncertainty. The chamber she found herself in was dimly lit, the air thick with the scent of ancient magic. Strange symbols glowed faintly on the walls, casting eerie shadows.

"Kael? Aric? Elara?" she called out, her voice echoing in the silence.

There was no response. Liora felt a surge of panic, but she forced herself to take a deep breath and focus. She could feel the amulet's steady pulse, its warmth a comforting presence against her skin.

"You can do this," she whispered to herself, her voice trembling. "You've come this far. Trust in yourself and the magic within you."

As she examined her surroundings, she noticed a series of intricate puzzles carved into the walls, each one glowing with a faint, magical light. They seemed to shift and change as she watched, presenting a new challenge with every moment.

"These are tests," Liora realized, her mind sharpening with determination. "I need to solve them to find my way back to the others."

Drawing on everything she had learned, Liora began to tackle the puzzles. Each one required a different combination of skills and knowledge—some demanded her understanding of ancient runes, others her intuition and connection to the amulet's magic.

As she worked, she felt her confidence growing, her fear slowly giving way to resolve. She was not alone; the amulet's magic and the support of her friends were with her, guiding her every step of the way.

Hours seemed to pass, the tests growing more complex and challenging. Sweat dripped down Liora's face, her muscles aching with exertion, but she refused to give up. She could feel the presence of her friends in her heart, their belief in her fueling her determination.

Finally, with a final, triumphant effort, she solved the last puzzle. The chamber around her began to shimmer and dissolve, revealing a hidden passage that led back to the main chamber.

Liora stepped through the passage, her heart racing with anticipation. She emerged to find Kael, Aric, and Elara waiting for her, their faces filled with relief and pride.

"Liora!" Kael exclaimed, rushing forward to embrace her. "We were so worried."

Aric nodded, his expression serious but warm. "You did it. You found your way back."

Elara's eyes glowed with approval. "Your strength and determination have brought you through. We are proud of you, Liora."

Tears filled Liora's eyes as she hugged her friends, their warmth and support a balm to her weary soul. "Thank you," she whispered, her voice filled with emotion. "I couldn't have done it without you."

They stood together, united in their resolve and ready to face whatever challenges lay ahead. The sanctuary had tested them, but they had emerged stronger, their bond unbreakable.

As they prepared to move forward, Liora felt a renewed sense of purpose. The Guardian Stone awaited, and with it, the power to protect their world from the encroaching darkness. They were ready to face the final ordeal, together.

With her friends by her side, Liora felt a renewed sense of strength and determination. They pressed on, moving deeper into the sanctuary. The air grew thicker with magic, and the walls seemed to hum with an ancient power. Each step brought them closer to the heart of the sanctum—and to the trials that awaited.

As they turned a corner, they found themselves at the entrance of a dark maze. The air within was cool and heavy, and strange whispers echoed from deep inside, making Liora's skin prickle.

"This is the Labyrinth of Shadows," Elara said, her voice barely above a whisper. "It's said to be filled with illusions designed to deceive and disorient."

Kael nodded, his expression serious. "We need to stay together and trust our instincts. Liora, you lead the way. The amulet will guide you."

Liora took a deep breath, feeling the comforting weight of the amulet against her chest. Its warmth steadied her, and she nodded. "I'll do my best. Stay close."

They entered the maze, the darkness swallowing them almost immediately. The walls seemed to shift and change, the path ahead winding unpredictably. Liora could hear the faint echo of their footsteps, the sound distorted and eerie.

As they moved deeper into the maze, the illusions began. Shadows flickered at the edge of her vision, taking on shapes that made her heart race—a figure from her past, a looming threat, a familiar face twisted with fear. She forced herself to focus, to trust the amulet's guidance.

The maze seemed to stretch on forever, each turn leading to new, disorienting challenges. At one point, the walls closed in around them, and the air grew thin. Liora felt a wave of panic, her breath coming in short gasps. She closed her eyes, trying to steady herself.

"Liora, focus," Kael's voice cut through the darkness, strong and reassuring. "We're with you."

She nodded, drawing strength from his words. She could feel the amulet's pulse, a steady beat that grounded her. With a deep breath, she opened her eyes and continued, her steps more confident.

Suddenly, the path ahead was blocked by a shimmering barrier of light. Liora paused, her brow furrowing. "What is this?"

Elara stepped forward, examining the barrier. "It's an illusion, but a powerful one. We need to dispel it to continue."

Liora felt a surge of frustration. They had come so far, and now they were being thwarted by a mere trick of the light. She clenched her fists, feeling the amulet's warmth intensify. A strange sensation washed over her, a tingling energy that seemed to flow from the amulet into her veins.

Without thinking, she raised her hand, focusing on the barrier. The energy surged through her, and to her astonishment, a beam of light shot from her fingertips, striking the barrier. The illusion shimmered and dissolved, revealing the path ahead.

"What... what was that?" Liora gasped, staring at her hand in shock.

Elara's eyes widened with awe. "You have a gift, Liora. The amulet has awakened a magical ability within you."

Kael smiled, his pride evident. "You're stronger than you realize, Liora. We all are."

Aric nodded, his expression serious but supportive. "We'll need that strength to get through this. Let's keep moving."

With newfound confidence, Liora led the way, the amulet's magic guiding her steps. The illusions grew more intense, but she faced them head-on, her fear giving way to determination. Each time the path seemed blocked, she drew on her newfound power, dispelling the illusions and clearing the way.

The maze twisted and turned, each step bringing them closer to the center. The air grew colder, the whispers louder, but Liora's resolve never wavered. She could feel the presence of her friends behind her, their support a constant source of strength.

Finally, after what felt like hours, they emerged from the maze into a vast, open chamber. The walls were lined with ancient runes, glowing faintly in the dim light. At the center of the chamber stood a pedestal, and on it rested a small, intricately carved box.

"This is it," Elara said, her voice filled with awe. "The heart of the Labyrinth."

Liora approached the pedestal, her heart pounding. The box seemed to pulse with energy, and she could feel the amulet's connection to it. She reached out, her fingers brushing the surface of the box.

As she opened it, a burst of light filled the chamber, and a voice echoed through the air. "You have proven your worth. The Guardian Stone awaits. But be warned, the final trial is yet to come."

Liora closed the box, her hand trembling. She turned to her friends, their faces reflecting the same mixture of awe and determination. "We're almost there. Together, we can face whatever comes next."

Kael placed a hand on her shoulder, his eyes filled with pride. "We're with you, Liora. Until the end."

Aric and Elara nodded, their resolve unwavering. They had faced the Labyrinth of Shadows and emerged stronger, their bond unbreakable. The final trial awaited, and they were ready to face it together.

They moved as one, stepping back into the labyrinth. This time, the path seemed clearer, the illusions weaker in the face of their combined strength. Liora led the way, the amulet's warmth a constant guide, its magic intertwined with her own newfound abilities.

As they navigated the final twists and turns of the maze, the air grew colder and more oppressive. Liora could feel the ancient magic of the sanctuary testing their resolve, probing their fears and doubts. But with each step, they grew stronger, their bond unbreakable.

Finally, they emerged from the labyrinth into a vast, open chamber. The walls were lined with glowing runes, casting a soft, ethereal light over the room. At the center of the chamber stood a pedestal, and on it rested the Guardian Stone. It pulsed with a radiant light, its energy filling the room with a sense of awe and reverence.

Liora's breath caught in her throat as she approached the pedestal, the amulet thrumming against her chest. She could feel the stone's power resonating with her, a deep, ancient magic that called to her very soul.

But between them and the Guardian Stone stood a final barrier—a shimmering wall of energy, crackling with raw power. Liora could feel its intensity, a tangible force that seemed to pulse with a life of its own.

"This is the final test," Elara said, her voice filled with awe. "We must find a way to dispel this barrier and claim the Guardian Stone."

Kael nodded, his eyes fixed on the barrier. "We've come this far. We can do this. Together."

Aric stepped forward, his expression determined. "Liora, you've led us through every challenge. We trust you. How do we get through this?"

Liora took a deep breath, focusing on the amulet's energy. She could feel its connection to the Guardian Stone, a thread of magic that bound them together. Closing her eyes, she let the magic flow through her, guiding her thoughts and actions.

"We need to combine our strengths," she said, opening her eyes. "The amulet's magic, Elara's spells, Kael's protection, and Aric's strength. Together, we can break the barrier."

Elara raised her staff, its light mingling with the glow of the amulet. "I'll channel my magic into the barrier, weakening its hold. Kael, protect us from any backlash."

Kael nodded, drawing his sword and positioning himself between the group and the barrier. "I'm ready."

Aric stepped beside Liora, his hand resting on the hilt of his sword. "Let's do this."

Liora focused on the amulet, feeling its warmth spread through her. She raised her hand, directing its energy toward the barrier. Elara began to chant, her voice a melodic incantation that filled the chamber with a resonant hum. Kael stood guard, his eyes sharp and vigilant, while Aric prepared to strike.

As the combined magic of the amulet and Elara's spells hit the barrier, it shimmered and pulsed, the energy crackling and sparking. Liora could feel the resistance, the raw power pushing back against them, but she held firm, drawing on the strength of her friends.

"Now, Aric!" Liora shouted, her voice strained with effort.

Aric stepped forward, his sword gleaming with a brilliant light. With a powerful swing, he struck the barrier, his blade slicing through the energy. The barrier shattered with a deafening roar, the force of the explosion sending shockwaves through the chamber.

Kael's protective shield held firm, deflecting the worst of the blast. As the dust settled, the barrier was gone, and the path to the Guardian Stone was clear.

Liora approached the pedestal, her heart pounding with anticipation. She reached out, her fingers brushing the cool, smooth surface of the stone. The Guardian Stone pulsed with a radiant light, its energy flowing into her, filling her with a sense of peace and power.

"We did it," she whispered, her voice filled with awe. "We've found the Guardian Stone."

Kael, Elara, and Aric joined her, their faces reflecting the same sense of triumph and relief. "This is just the beginning," Kael said, his voice steady. "We've claimed the Guardian Stone, but we must still protect it and use its power to repel the darkness."

Chapter 8: The Reward

Liora stood before the Guardian Stone, its radiant light bathing her in a warm, ethereal glow. The stone pulsed with an ancient power, its energy flowing through her, filling her with a sense of peace and immense strength. As her fingers brushed its cool surface, she felt a surge of knowledge and understanding flood her mind.

Her vision blurred, and the world around her dissolved into a swirling vortex of light and shadow. She closed her eyes, letting the magic of the Guardian Stone envelop her. When she opened them again, she found herself standing in a vast, open plain, the sky above filled with storm clouds and crackling lightning.

Before her stood a grand city, its towers reaching towards the heavens, bathed in a golden light. But the city was under siege, dark forces battering its walls and swarming its streets. Shadowy figures, twisted and monstrous, fought against warriors clad in shining armor. The air was thick with the sounds of battle—clashing swords, roaring beasts, and the cries of the wounded.

Liora watched, her heart pounding, as the scene unfolded. She saw a figure standing at the center of the chaos, a tall, imposing man with eyes that burned like fire. He wielded a dark, twisted staff, its tip crackling with malevolent energy. She recognized him instantly: the Shadow Lord from her vision.

"This is the beginning," a voice whispered in her mind, ancient and wise. "The origin of the darkness that now threatens your world."

The vision shifted, and Liora saw the same figure, now kneeling before a massive, dark crystal embedded in the ground. The crystal pulsed with a sinister light, its energy corrupting everything around it. The man's eyes glowed with an intense, unnatural fire as he chanted an incantation, his voice echoing through the air.

"This crystal is the source of the Shadow Lord's power," the voice continued. "He draws his strength from its dark energy, and through it, he commands the forces of darkness."

The vision shifted again, and Liora saw the Guardian Stone, its light a beacon of hope amidst the encroaching darkness. She saw a group of warriors and mages standing before it, their faces determined and resolute. They raised their hands, channeling their magic into the stone, and its light grew brighter, pushing back the shadows.

"These were the guardians of old," the voice said. "They used the power of the Guardian Stone to protect their world, just as you must do now."

Liora felt a surge of determination and purpose. She understood now the true nature of the dark force they were fighting against. The Shadow Lord's power came from the dark crystal, and only by using the Guardian Stone could they hope to repel him and save their world.

The vision began to fade, and Liora felt herself being pulled back to the present. The light of the Guardian Stone surrounded her, filling her with its strength and knowledge. She opened her eyes, finding herself once again in the sanctuary, her friends standing around her, their faces filled with concern and anticipation.

"Liora, are you alright?" Kael asked, his voice steady but worried.

Liora nodded, her heart still racing from the intensity of the vision. "I'm alright. The Guardian Stone showed me the past—the true nature of the dark force we're fighting."

Elara stepped forward, her violet eyes glowing with curiosity. "What did you see?"

Liora took a deep breath, gathering her thoughts. "The Shadow Lord draws his power from a dark crystal, a source of immense and corrupting energy. He uses it to command the forces of darkness. The only way to defeat him is to use the power of the Guardian Stone."

Aric's expression grew serious. "Then we need to find this dark crystal and destroy it."

Kael nodded, his face filled with determination. "The Guardian Stone has given us the knowledge and the power we need. Now it's up to us to act."

Liora felt a surge of resolve, the weight of their mission settling over her. "We need to return to the village and prepare. The final battle is coming, and we must be ready."

Chapter 9: The Road Back

The first light of dawn cast a golden hue over the forest as Liora, Kael, Aric, and Elara prepared to leave the sanctuary. The Guardian Stone, safely secured in Liora's satchel, pulsed with a steady, reassuring light. The air was thick with tension, knowing that Malakar's forces would soon be upon them.

"We need to move quickly," Kael said, his voice low and urgent. "Malakar's forces won't rest until they have the Guardian Stone. We must stay ahead of them."

Liora nodded, her heart pounding with a mix of fear and determination. The weight of the Guardian Stone was both a burden and a source of strength. She could feel its power resonating with her own, giving her the resolve to face the challenges ahead.

As they fled the sanctuary, the forest seemed to close in around them, the shadows deepening with every step. The once familiar paths were now fraught with danger, each turn potentially leading to an ambush. The sound of distant howls echoed through the trees, a chilling reminder of the relentless pursuit behind them.

"Stay close and keep your eyes sharp," Aric said, his voice a low growl. "We need to find a safe route back to the village."

Elara raised her staff, its light casting a protective glow around them. "I'll sense any magical traps or barriers ahead. We can't afford to be caught off guard."

They moved swiftly through the forest, navigating treacherous terrain and dense underbrush. The ground was uneven, covered in roots and fallen leaves that made each step a careful calculation. Liora could feel the adrenaline coursing through her veins, her senses heightened and alert.

As they reached a narrow ravine, the sound of rushing water filled the air. The only way across was a series of slippery, moss-covered rocks. Kael tested the first rock with his foot, then nodded. "We need to cross quickly but carefully. One slip, and we could be swept away."

Liora took a deep breath and stepped onto the first rock, feeling it shift slightly under her weight. She moved with deliberate precision, her heart pounding with each step. Behind her, Kael, Aric, and Elara followed, their movements synchronized and cautious.

Halfway across, a sudden roar echoed through the ravine. Liora's eyes widened in alarm as she saw a group of shadowy figures emerging from the trees on the opposite side. Malakar's minions had found them.

"Move faster!" Kael shouted, his voice filled with urgency.

Liora quickened her pace, her feet barely touching the slippery rocks as she leaped from one to the next. The roar of the water grew louder, the current threatening to pull them under. She felt a surge of panic but forced herself to stay focused, the amulet's warmth a steady reminder of their mission.

As they reached the other side, the shadowy figures closed in, their eyes glowing with malevolent intent. Aric drew his sword, his face set in grim determination. "We'll hold them off. Liora, get the Guardian Stone to safety."

Liora hesitated, her heart torn. She didn't want to leave her friends behind, but she knew the Guardian Stone was their only hope. "Be careful," she whispered, her voice trembling with emotion.

Kael placed a reassuring hand on her shoulder. "We'll be right behind you. Go."

With a final, determined nod, Liora turned and fled into the forest, the Guardian Stone's light guiding her way. She could hear the sounds of battle behind her, the clash of swords and the roar of magic. Tears filled her eyes, but she pressed on, driven by the knowledge that she had to protect the Guardian Stone at all costs.

As she navigated the dense forest, the terrain grew even more treacherous. The ground was uneven, the trees thick and twisted. She could feel the presence of Malakar's forces, their dark energy a constant threat. But the amulet's warmth and the light of the Guardian Stone gave her strength, pushing her forward.

Liora stumbled over a root, her breath coming in ragged gasps. She paused for a moment, leaning against a tree to catch her breath. The forest was silent now, the sounds of battle distant but still echoing in her mind.

She closed her eyes, focusing on the amulet's pulse. "Guide me," she whispered, feeling a surge of energy flow through her. She opened her eyes, a renewed sense of determination filling her.

As she continued through the forest, she noticed a faint, shimmering path appear before her. The amulet's magic was showing her the way, leading her through the maze of trees and underbrush. She followed the path, her steps quick and sure.

Finally, she emerged into a small clearing, the sunlight filtering through the trees in golden beams. She could feel the amulet's energy intensify, a sign that she was on the right track. But as she stepped forward, a shadow fell across the clearing.

Malakar stood before her, his eyes burning with fury. "You've caused me enough trouble, girl," he snarled. "Give me the Guardian Stone, and I might spare your life."

Liora's heart pounded, but she stood her ground, drawing on the amulet's strength. "I won't let you take it," she said, her voice steady. "You'll have to go through me."

Malakar laughed, a cruel, mocking sound. "So be it."

He raised his staff, dark energy crackling around it. Liora felt a surge of fear but quickly pushed it aside, focusing on the amulet's power. She raised her hand, a beam of light shooting from her fingertips and clashing with Malakar's dark magic.

The clearing erupted in a blaze of light and shadow, the forces of good and evil clashing with a thunderous roar. Liora could feel the strain, the amulet's energy pulsing through her with an intensity she had never felt before. She gritted her teeth, pushing back against Malakar's power with everything she had.

Suddenly, a figure burst into the clearing, sword raised. Kael's blade struck Malakar's staff, shattering it with a flash of light. Malakar screamed, the dark energy dissipating around him.

Aric and Elara followed, their faces filled with determination. Together, they surrounded Malakar, their combined strength overwhelming him. With a final, furious roar, Malakar dissolved into shadows, disappearing into the forest.

Liora fell to her knees, her breath coming in ragged gasps. Kael was at her side in an instant, his hand on her shoulder. "Are you alright?"

She nodded, tears streaming down her face. "I'm fine. Thanks to you."

Elara knelt beside her, her violet eyes filled with concern. "We need to keep moving. Malakar may be gone for now, but his forces will regroup."

Aric sheathed his sword, his expression serious. "We need to get the Guardian Stone to the village. It's our only hope."

Liora took a deep breath, feeling the amulet's warmth and the light of the Guardian Stone filling her with strength. "Let's go," she said, her voice steady. "Together."

They moved through the forest as one, their bond unbreakable. The journey was far from over, but they were ready to face whatever challenges lay ahead. With the Guardian Stone's power and their united strength, they would protect their world from the darkness and ensure that the light would shine forever.

The edge of the forest was within sight, the golden fields of Eldergrove just beyond the treeline. Liora felt a surge of hope and relief as they neared their home. The Guardian Stone pulsed with a comforting light, its power a beacon of hope. But as they stepped into the clearing at the forest's edge, that hope was shattered.

Malakar stood waiting for them, his eyes burning with malevolent fury. Around him were more of his minions, their dark forms shifting and writhing in the shadows. The air crackled with dark energy, and a sense of foreboding filled Liora's heart.

"You cannot escape me," Malakar hissed, his voice echoing through the clearing. "The Guardian Stone will be mine, and your world will fall into darkness."

Kael stepped forward, his sword raised, eyes filled with determination. "We won't let you take it, Malakar. This ends now."

The battle erupted with a fury that took Liora's breath away. Kael and Aric charged at Malakar's minions, their swords flashing in the dim light. Elara raised her staff, casting protective spells and striking down the dark creatures with bursts of magical energy. Liora felt the Guardian Stone's power surge within her, and she focused its energy, sending beams of light towards their enemies.

Malakar laughed, his dark magic clashing with their combined forces. "You are fools to think you can stand against me!"

Liora felt a wave of fear but quickly pushed it aside. She raised her hand, channeling the Guardian Stone's power, and directed it towards Malakar. A beam of radiant light shot from her fingers, striking him with a force that shook the ground.

Malakar staggered but quickly regained his footing, his eyes blazing with anger. He raised his staff, dark energy swirling around it, and launched a counterattack. The force of his magic struck Kael, sending him crashing to the ground.

"No!" Liora screamed, her heart breaking as she saw Kael's motionless form. She ran to his side, her hands trembling as she reached for him. "Kael, please, get up!"

Kael's eyes fluttered open, and he looked up at her with a weak smile. "Liora, you have to keep fighting. Protect the Guardian Stone. You can do this."

Tears streamed down Liora's face as she nodded, her resolve hardening. She felt the Guardian Stone's power flow through her, filling her with strength and determination. "I won't let you down, Kael. I promise."

She stood, her eyes blazing with fury and determination. Malakar watched her, his expression one of twisted amusement. "You think you can defeat me, girl? You are nothing compared to my power."

Liora raised her hand, the Guardian Stone's light glowing brightly. "I am not alone," she said, her voice steady. "We are stronger together."

She focused all her energy on the Guardian Stone, feeling its power surge through her. The light grew brighter, enveloping her in a radiant glow. She directed the energy towards Malakar, the beam of light piercing through the darkness.

Malakar screamed, the force of the light overwhelming him. His dark energy clashed with the Guardian Stone's power, but Liora's determination was unyielding. She pushed forward, her friends' strength and support guiding her.

With a final, deafening roar, Malakar was consumed by the light, his form disintegrating into shadows. The dark minions dissolved into the air, leaving the clearing silent and still.

Liora fell to her knees, the exhaustion of the battle washing over her. She turned to Kael, who lay motionless on the ground. Elara and Aric rushed to his side, their faces filled with worry and grief.

"Kael," Elara whispered, her voice trembling. "Stay with us."

Kael's eyes opened briefly, and he looked at them with a faint smile. "You did it," he said, his voice weak. "You saved us all."

Liora took his hand, tears streaming down her face. "You can't leave us, Kael. We need you."

Kael's grip tightened briefly before he closed his eyes, his breathing slowing. "Protect the Guardian Stone," he murmured. "Together."

His hand went limp, and Liora felt a wave of grief crash over her. She sobbed, holding his hand tightly, her heart breaking.

Elara placed a gentle hand on Liora's shoulder, her own eyes filled with tears. "We must honor his sacrifice. We have to protect the Guardian Stone and ensure his death was not in vain."

Aric's face was set in grim determination. "We will make sure his sacrifice was not in vain. We'll protect the Guardian Stone and defeat the darkness."

Liora nodded, her grief turning into a fierce resolve. She felt the weight of the Guardian Stone in her hands, its power a reminder of their mission. "We will protect our world," she said, her voice steady. "For Kael."

As they made their way back to the village, the light of the Guardian Stone guiding their path, Liora felt a renewed sense of purpose. They had lost a dear friend, but his sacrifice would not be forgotten. Together, they would honor his memory and ensure that the light of the Guardian Stone would shine forever, protecting their world from the darkness.

The grief of Kael's loss hung heavily over the group as they moved through the forest, the weight of their mission intensified by their sorrow. The Guardian Stone pulsed gently in Liora's satchel, its light a somber reminder of the power they carried and the sacrifices that had been made.

Chapter 10: Return with the Elixir

The journey back to Eldergrove was filled with a quiet, solemn determination. Liora, Aric, and Elara moved through the forest with a newfound sense of purpose. The Guardian Stone, now safely secured and pulsing gently, guided their way. The memory of Kael's sacrifice lingered in their hearts, a poignant reminder of the cost of their mission.

As they approached the village, the first rays of dawn cast a golden light over the fields. The air was crisp and fresh, filled with the sounds of birds awakening to the new day. The sight of Eldergrove, untouched by the darkness, filled Liora with a deep sense of relief and gratitude.

"We're almost home," Elara said softly, her violet eyes shimmering with a mixture of sadness and hope. "The village is safe."

Liora nodded, her heart swelling with emotion. "We did it. We protected the Guardian Stone and our world."

As they entered the village, the sight of the returning heroes brought the villagers rushing to greet them. Faces filled with worry and anticipation lit up with joy and relief. The children, who had been kept safe in the village hall, ran out to embrace their parents, their laughter echoing through the streets.

Mara, the village elder, approached them, her eyes filled with tears of gratitude. "You've returned," she said, her voice trembling with emotion. "You've saved us all."

Liora stepped forward, holding the Guardian Stone aloft. Its light bathed the village in a gentle glow, a symbol of their victory and the power they had fought to protect. "The dark force has been repelled for now," she announced, her voice strong and clear. "The Guardian Stone's power will help to protect us."

The villagers cheered, their voices filled with relief and joy. Liora felt a surge of pride and gratitude as she looked at her friends. Aric stood tall, his eyes reflecting the strength and determination that had carried them through. Elara's face was serene, her expression filled with quiet pride.

Mara placed a hand on Liora's shoulder, her eyes filled with wisdom and kindness. "You've done more than protect the village, Liora. You've shown us all the power of unity and courage. Kael's spirit will live on in your deeds."

Liora felt tears well up in her eyes, but she smiled, feeling a sense of peace. "Kael's sacrifice gave us the strength to succeed. We will honor his memory by protecting our home and each other."

As the village celebrated, Liora, Aric, and Elara made their way to the central square. They placed the Guardian Stone on a pedestal, its light casting a protective aura over the entire village. The air seemed to hum with the magic of the stone, a constant reminder of their victory and the power they now safeguarded.

"We need to ensure the Guardian Stone remains protected," Aric said, his voice steady. "Malakar may be weak for now, but he will be back stronger than ever so we must stay vigilant."

Elara nodded, her eyes thoughtful. "We will establish a guard and set wards around the village. The Guardian Stone's power is a beacon of hope, but also a target. We must be ready for anything."

Liora looked at her friends, feeling a deep sense of unity and purpose. "Together, we will protect our world. The darkness has been pushed back, but we must remain strong. For Kael, and for all of us."

The village buzzed with activity as preparations were made to safeguard the Guardian Stone. Wards were set, and a guard was established to watch over the stone day and night. The villagers worked together, their bond strengthened by the trials they had faced.

As night fell, the village gathered around the Guardian Stone. Liora stood with Aric and Elara, their hearts filled with a mixture of sorrow and triumph. The light of the stone bathed them in its gentle glow, a testament to their courage and unity.

"We have faced the darkness and emerged victorious," Liora said, her voice carrying through the silent night. "We will honor those we lost by protecting the light. Together, we are strong."

The villagers cheered, their voices filled with hope and determination. Liora felt a sense of peace settle over her, the weight of their journey lifted by the strength of their unity. They had returned with the elixir, the Guardian Stone's power, and the knowledge that together, they could face anything.

She closed her eyes, reflecting on the path that had brought her here. From a young herbalist in a small village to the bearer of the Guardian Stone, she had grown in ways she could never have imagined. She thought of Kael, his wisdom and courage guiding her even now. His sacrifice had not been in vain, and she was determined to honor his memory by continuing to protect their world.

Elara approached her, her footsteps soft on the grass. "You've come a long way, Liora," she said, her voice gentle. "We all have. But you especially."

Liora opened her eyes and smiled, feeling a deep sense of gratitude. "I couldn't have done it without you and Aric. We're a team. And together, we're unstoppable."

Elara nodded, her violet eyes glowing softly in the darkness. "The journey may have changed us, but it has also made us stronger. The Guardian Stone's power is a testament to that strength. And so are you, Liora."

Aric joined them, his presence solid and reassuring. "What now?" he asked, his voice steady. "The village is safe, but there are still threats out there. The world needs protectors."

Liora looked at her friends, feeling a surge of determination. "We've only just begun. The Guardian Stone is safe here, but there's so much more to explore and protect. I need to understand my newfound powers better, and we need to be ready for whatever comes next."

Elara smiled, her expression filled with pride. "Then let's continue our journey. There's a whole world out there that needs us."

Aric nodded, his eyes reflecting the same determination. "We'll stand by you, Liora. Wherever this path leads, we'll face it together."

Liora felt a sense of excitement and purpose. The journey that had started with a simple quest to protect her village had transformed into something much greater. She had discovered strengths within herself that she never knew existed, and she had forged bonds that would last a lifetime.

As they stood together, the first light of dawn began to break on the horizon, casting a golden glow over Eldergrove. It was a new day, a new beginning. And Liora was ready to embrace it.

She turned to the Guardian Stone, its light a constant reminder of their victory and the power they now held. "We will protect this land," she said, her voice filled with resolve. "And we will continue to grow, to learn, and to fight for what is right. For Kael, for our village, and for the future."

Elara and Aric placed their hands on the stone, their expressions filled with the same determination. "Together," Elara said, her voice strong. "We are the guardians."

Liora nodded, feeling a deep sense of unity and purpose. "Together," she echoed.

As the sun rose, casting its light over the village and the forest beyond, Liora felt a renewed sense of hope and determination. The journey ahead was filled with unknowns, but she knew they were ready. They had faced the darkness and emerged stronger for it. And whatever challenges lay ahead, they would face them together.

With the Guardian Stone's power and the strength of their unity, they would protect their world and ensure that the light of hope would never fade. Their adventure was far from over. In fact, it was only just beginning. And Liora was ready to embrace the future, with her friends by her side and the power of the Guardian Stone guiding their way.

Together, they would explore new horizons, uncover ancient secrets, and protect their land from any threat. The journey continued, and Liora knew that as long as they stood together, they could face anything.

And so, with the dawn of a new day, Liora, Aric, and Elara set out to discover what lay beyond the horizon, their hearts filled with hope and determination, ready for whatever adventures awaited them.

Get Another Book Free

We love writing and have produced many books.

As a thank you for being one of our amazing readers, we'd like to offer you a free book.

To claim this limited-time offer, visit the site below and enter your name and email address.

You'll receive one of our great books directly to your email, completely free!

https://free.copypeople.com

---

1. https://free.copypeople.com

Also by Sable Moonshadow

The Guardian Stone
Legends of the Guardian Stone

www.ingramcontent.com/pod-product-compliance
Lightning Source LLC
Chambersburg PA
CBHW052121150726
48002CB00006B/2448